P9-CFQ-960

Hyperion and the Great Balls of Fire

DON'T MISS THE OTHER ADVENTURES IN THE HEROES IN TRAINING SERIES!

Zeus and the Thunderbolt of Doom

Poseidon and the Sea of Fury

Hades and the Helm of Darkness

COMING SOON:

Typhon and the Winds of Destruction

HEROES IN TRAINING

Hyperion and the Great Balls of Fire

Joan Holub and
Suzanne Williams

Aladdin
NEW YORK LONDON TORONTO SYDNEY NEW DELHI

If you purchased this book without a cover, you should be aware that this book is stolen property. It was reported as "unsold and destroyed" to the publisher, and neither the author nor the publisher has received any payment for this "stripped book."

This book is a work of fiction. Any references to historical events, real people, or real places are used fictitiously. Other names, characters, places, and events are products of the authors' imagination, and any resemblance to actual events or places or persons, living or dead, is entirely coincidental.

ALADDIN
An imprint of Simon & Schuster Children's Publishing Division
1230 Avenue of the Americas, New York, NY 10020
First Aladdin paperback edition August 2013
Text copyright © 2013 by Joan Holub and Suzanne Williams
Illustrations copyright © 2013 by Craig Phillips
All rights reserved, including the right of reproduction
in whole or in part in any form.
ALADDIN is a trademark of Simon & Schuster, Inc.,
and related logo is a registered trademark of Simon & Schuster, Inc.
Also available in an Aladdin hardcover edition.
For information about special discounts for bulk purchases,
please contact Simon & Schuster Special Sales
at 1-866-506-1949 or business@simonandschuster.com.
The Simon & Schuster Speakers Bureau can bring authors to your live event.
For more information or to book an event,
contact the Simon & Schuster Speakers Bureau at 1-866-248-3049
or visit our website at www.simonspeakers.com.
Designed by Karin Paprocki
The text of this book was set in Adobe Garamond Pro.
Manufactured in the United States of America 0713 OFF
2 4 6 8 10 9 7 5 3 1
Library of Congress Control Number 2012943206
ISBN 978-1-4424-5269-5 (pbk)
ISBN 978-1-4424-5803-1 (hc)
ISBN 978-1-4424-5270-1 (eBook)

For our heroic readers
—J. H. and S. W.

Contents

Hyperion and the Great Balls of Fire

Greetings, Mortal Readers,

I am Pythia, the Oracle of Delphi, in Greece. I have the power to see the future. Hear my prophecy:

Ahead I see dancers lurking. Wait—make that *danger* lurking. (The future can be blurry, especially when my eyeglasses are foggy.)

Anyhoo, beware! Titan giants now rule all of Earth's domains—oceans, mountains, forests, and the depths of the Underwear. Oops—make that *Underworld*. Led by King Cronus, they are out to destroy us all!

Yet I foresee hope. A band of rightful rulers called Olympians will arise. Though their size and youth are no match for the Titans, they will be giant in heart, mind, and spirit. They await their leader—a very special yet clueless boy. One who is destined to become king of the gods and ruler of the heavens.

If he is brave enough.

And if he can get his friends to work together. And if they can learn to use their new amazing flowers—um, amazing *powers*—in time to save the world!

CHAPTER ONE

Boom! Boom! Boom!

K*a-BOOM! Sssst!*

A fireball as big as a watermelon struck the ground and exploded in flames. It had landed only a few feet from Zeus! He and four other ten-year-old Olympians had all been sleeping in a small forest at the edge of an abandoned village.

"Yeee-ikes!" yelled Zeus. Instantly wide awake, he leaped to his feet.

"My sandal's on fire!" shouted Hades, hopping around.

"I'm on it!" Poseidon called. He lifted his golden trident, which looked sort of like a pitchfork—only cooler.

Whoosh! Three streams of water suddenly spurted from the three pointy tips of the trident, hitting Hades' foot. It was just enough to put out the sandal fire.

Hades looked from Poseidon to the trident in surprise. "Did you gain a new magical power when I wasn't looking?"

Poseidon nodded. "My trident can magically draw water from any source nearby. A lake, a pond, even from deep underground. I figured it out last night when I was wishing for a drink of water."

"Handy trick," said Hera. She and Demeter—the two girl Olympians—had woken as well.

"Especially since those fireballs are back again," added Demeter.

All five Olympians had been dodging the mysterious fireballs since the day before. However, for some reason the attacks had stopped at sundown last night.

Now that it was dawn, the sun was here again. And so were the fireballs.

"I think the Titans are playing some evil game with us," said Poseidon.

Screee!

"Like Dodge the Fireball? Let's get out of here!" yelled Hera as another flaming ball came screaming in.

BOOM! Sssst!

The Olympians took off just in time. They hurdled over rocks and raced across parched ground. *If only there were a finish line somewhere,* thought Zeus. A place where they'd finally be safe from harm. Was that only wishful thinking?

The future is what you make of it, Pythia the Oracle had told them. *If and when all of the Olympians are united again, you will have the power to defeat Cronus and his evil ways.*

It was because of her that they'd begun yet another quest. This time they'd been sent to find the Olympic Torch. But as usual with the oracle's quests, she hadn't given them any details. Such as what the torch looked like. Or who had it. Or why it was important to find it.

Screee! BOOM! Sssst! Another fiery ball struck the dirt right behind Zeus. A huge plume of fire and smoke shot up from the ground.

"Thunderation!" he yelled. Flames licked at his heels as he put on a burst of speed.

"Someone's trying to blast us to smithereens!" shouted Hades.

"Yeah," Zeus said, panting. "And I think I might know who that someone is."

"Who?" Hera called out. She and Demeter were right behind them.

Poseidon came last. Pausing, he aimed the tips of his trident at the spot where the last fireball had fallen. A spurt of water put out the fire.

Screee! Boom! Sssst! Another fireball landed to the right of the Olympians.

They veered down a road that went left. "Look. A temple!" shouted Zeus. He pointed to a white marble building surrounded by columns. It stood at the bottom of a hill. "Let's take shelter there."

Soon the Olympians were all safely inside the temple. Hera shoved back a lock of long, golden hair that had fallen over her face. "Okay, Thunderboy," she said to Zeus. "So who's after us?"

The irritation in her voice was impossible to miss. At least she hadn't called him Thunder-*pants*. Another of her many nicknames for him.

Zeus shrugged. "It's only a guess. But I think it could be the work of one of the Titans I saw with Cronus. That day I made him barf."

Until recently the other four Olympians had all been imprisoned in the belly of the evil King Cronus. But after Zeus had sent a thunderbolt down the giant Titan king's throat, the king had barfed them all up.

Unfortunately, most of them had been recaptured by the Titans. They'd had to be rescued all over again, one by one. Zeus had seen to that.

But there was still another Olympian left to rescue. A girl named Hestia.

"The Titan I'm thinking of has a head that glows like the sun," said Zeus.

"Hyperion!" Demeter exclaimed, her green

eyes flashing. "That would make sense. He's the Titan god of light. The physical incarnation of the sun."

"The fizzy-calling-car what?" asked Poseidon.

Hera rolled her eyes. "Duh. It means he sort of *is* the sun. In bodily form."

They all ducked as they heard another fireball hit the ground somewhere outside.

"Does he hurl fireballs—er, sunballs?" Hades asked.

Zeus looked around for Hades but didn't see him. He must've put on his Helm of Darkness. It was a jeweled crown that made him invisible.

"Maybe," Zeus replied. "But no matter *who* is after us, we still have an Olympic Torch to find." He stood up and went to peek out one of the temple's windows.

"I'm betting that when we do find it, we'll also find Hestia," said Poseidon. "Because remember what the oracle told us: 'Find the torch, and you will also find more of those you seek.'"

"Right," said Hera. "Pythia also said the torch belongs to the Protector of the Hearth. Maybe that's *me*."

"Or me," Demeter said evenly. Both girls were a little annoyed that the boys all had magical objects. Zeus had a lightning bolt. Poseidon, a trident. And Hades, a helm. Yet the girls still had nothing.

Zeus patted the small thunderbolt tucked under his belt. It sparked at his touch. Although many had tried before him, only he had managed to pull it from the big cone-shaped stone in Pythia's temple. It was dagger-size now, but he could make it five feet long if he wanted.

"You know, I used to think my bolt belonged to someone named *Goose*," he told the others. At the silly name, Poseidon snickered and Hades smirked. The girls grinned.

"Only because that's what Pythia said the first time I met her," Zeus added quickly. "But it looks like she meant me all the time."

Demeter nodded. "*Goose. Zeus.* They'd be easy to confuse. Sounds like it was just another of her foggy-spectacle mistakes."

Yes, thought Zeus. And that meant the thunderbolt was really and truly his. It also meant he was the *leader* of the Olympians. Pythia had said so. He wasn't sure he *wanted* to be their leader. But since it was his destiny, he'd try to do his best.

Suddenly, loud shouts, heavy footsteps, and the clank of armor alerted the five Olympians to danger.

"Soldiers are coming!" hissed Hades' disembodied voice. "I can see them out front through the window."

Everyone looked at Zeus. "Should we fight them or run?" asked Poseidon.

Zeus hesitated. With their magical objects the boys could most likely ward off the Cronies. (That was what everyone called King Cronus's soldiers.) They might even be able to make the soldiers retreat.

"What? No answer, Mr. Smarty Thunder-pants?" Hera asked.

Argh! There she went with those nicknames again, thought Zeus.

"Better if we escape before the Cronies figure out we're here," he decided. "Less risk of being captured or followed."

He could see daylight shining in through a hole at the bottom of the back temple wall. The hole was singed around the edges. Probably made by a fireball hitting the temple. And it looked just big enough for them to wiggle through.

"We can go out through that hole. Hurry!"

CHAPTER TWO

The Missing Torch

Zeus was last to escape out the fireball hole. And just in time too. As he wriggled through, he heard the Cronies. They were stomping up the front steps of the temple.

"Let's check in here!" he heard one of them shout.

It was Lion Tattoo! Zeus realized. He was the leader of the three half-giants who'd kidnapped Zeus in Crete. Zeus had escaped them more than once. Good thing too, since they were always threatening to fry, grill, or toast him for a snack!

Once Zeus was outside, he raced to join his friends. Lucky for him none of the soldiers had come around to the back of the temple. Yet. But up ahead his fellow Olympians were nowhere in sight.

"This way!" a voice whispered. Hera sprang up from behind a large boulder, surprising him.

Zeus grinned at her. "Waiting for me?" he asked.

She rolled her eyes. "*Someone* had to, Boltbrain. So you wouldn't get lost."

Boltbrain? That was a new one, thought Zeus.

Together they took off running. They had to hop over lots of big dents in the road where fireballs had struck. The temple was soon lost to view as they rounded a hill.

Spotting Hades, Poseidon, and Demeter up ahead, Zeus and Hera caught up to them. From there they all wandered through one empty village after another. The farther they traveled, the more the sun beat down. It baked everything it touched.

After a while they came upon yet another small village. It looked as abandoned as all the rest.

Hera peeked in a door that someone had left open. "Hello? Anybody home?" she called out.

"They left. Wouldn't you? This place is fried," said Poseidon, fanning himself.

Demeter bent to stroke the leaves of a withered wildflower. "Poor little thing," she said. At her touch the purple flower perked up on its stem a little. When she let go, it wilted again.

Seeing this, Zeus's eyes widened. Was her touch somehow magic?

"Look! A water well!" Poseidon yelled. He

ran ahead to the well in the village center and looked inside it. Then his shoulders drooped. "It's empty."

Zeus hadn't realized how thirsty he was until now. Occasional sips of water from Poseidon's trident weren't enough. He went over to stare down into the well too.

"Can you fill it?" he asked.

"I'll try," said Poseidon. Holding tight to the handle of his trident, he lowered its three-pointed end over the side of the well. "Long!" he commanded. Instantly the trident began to lengthen.

When its sharp prongs reached the bottom of the well, Poseidon commanded it to drill. Spinning in superfast circles, the trident obeyed. It drilled down through the earth, going deeper and deeper. Minutes later water bubbled up, swiftly filling the well.

"Hooray!" Hera grabbed a terra-cotta jug from several that sat beside the well. She filled the jug with water and took a long drink. Then she passed it around to the others.

"Flippin' fish lips! That's good!" Poseidon declared when it was his turn to quench his thirst.

"Better than the water from the River Lethe?" Zeus asked. Poseidon had drunk half a glass of water from that Underworld river during their last quest. It had temporarily made him forget half of everything he knew.

"Huh? What River Lethe?" Poseidon joked now. "I don't remember it."

Zeus and the others laughed.

"Shh," Hades said suddenly. "I hear something."

The five Olympians froze. Zeus's eyes scanned the far end of the village road. He expected to see Cronies. But instead a group of tired travelers appeared.

"Water!" one of them shouted. The whole bunch of them swarmed the well. They grabbed jugs and scooped up water, then drank thirstily.

"My village ran out of water a week ago," a man in a blue shirt explained.

A woman nodded. "There's a drought where I live in Olympia, too. Hyperion took over a temple there. He's been scorching every village and farm field for miles around."

Zeus's eyebrows shot up at the mention of Hyperion's name. So he'd been right to suspect the sun-headed Titan!

More travelers came, including a family. The young children ran to look at Poseidon's trident. He twirled it over their heads. They squealed with delight as a shower of cooling water drops rained down over them.

"Where did you get that thing?" their father asked. "Is it magic? Rumor has it that Hyperion is collecting magical objects. For King Cronus."

"Heard he's already captured a magical flame," another man added before Poseidon could reply. "Now his soldiers are searching every temple in Greece for a magical torch that can hold it."

So that's why the Cronies had stormed the temple he and the others had hidden in, thought Zeus. They'd been after the magical torch, not the Olympians, for once! He wondered if the flame's and the torch's magic somehow became stronger when they were together. A package deal.

"Maybe that's why Hyperion started throwing fireballs," Zeus murmured, thinking aloud. "Hoping to scare someone into fessing up about where the missing torch is."

"Any idea where it might be?" Hera asked the men.

Zeus knew what she must be thinking. That they should try to find it before Hyperion did.

Of course, Hera was convinced that she was the Protector of the Hearth, the Olympian that Pythia had spoken of in her prophecy. Which would mean the Olympic Torch would be Hera's magical object.

But Demeter was just as sure that the prophecy referred to *her*. Unfortunately, only one of them could be right.

"No one knows," said a woman in answer to Hera's question. "But once Hyperion has both flame and torch, he'll surely give them to Cronus. Who will turn their use to evil. Like he does everything else."

"Fireballs!" someone yelled suddenly. Everyone fled as three great balls of fire screamed down from the sky.

Zeus jumped over a low stone wall. He flattened himself against the trunk of a giant oak tree.

Just then the amulet that hung on a cord around his neck twitched against his skin. He pulled the smooth chip of stone from the throat of his tunic. The chip was as big as his fist. Like his thunderbolt it had come from the temple in Delphi where he'd first met Pythia the Oracle.

The other Olympians soon joined him in his hiding place. The five of them huddled together under the oak tree. They peered at the chip as the symbols that were now scattered across its surface arranged themselves into a map.

A small black arrow appeared on the map. It pointed toward a red dot labeled OLYMPIA.

"Flyin' fish sticks," said Poseidon. "That's where Hyperion is holed up! We have to go *there*?"

"Mm-hm," said Zeus. The chip guided them on all their quests. They followed wherever it led.

"But even if we *do* manage to steal the magical

flame from him, we'll need the torch, too, right?" said Hades. "Sounds like the flame must not work right without it."

"One of the villagers I gave water to told me about a temple south of here," Hera said, sounding excited. "Inside it there's a torch that refuses to light. I think it could be the Olympic Torch!"

"Maybe," said Zeus. "But Chip is pointing us to *Olympia*. In the north. Seems more likely the *Olympic* Torch would be there. If it's not, Chip will probably tell us where to find it. After we get the flame from Hyperion."

But as usual Hera disagreed with his plans. "By then it might be too late," she argued. "The Cronies are already hunting for the torch. They might beat us to it."

"How about if we split up?" Demeter suggested. "Hera and I can go south and look for the torch at that temple. You guys can go north and steal the flame."

"I think we should all stay together," said Zeus. "You don't have weapons. How would you defend—"

"Exactly!" Hera crowed. "Without weapons or magic of our own, Demeter and I can't help you against Hyperion. So you won't need us."

She had a point, thought Zeus. "All right, then," he said, seeing some wisdom in her plan. "Be careful, though."

"Humpf," said Hera, tossing her long golden hair. "We can take care of ourselves."

"Sure," quipped Poseidon. "Like on our last quest when you got captured and taken to the Underworld?"

Hera's face flushed red. But before she could think of a snappy comeback, another fireball came sizzling down from the sky.

Boom! Ssssst!

Crack! It hit the giant oak tree, splitting it. As the tree toppled, the Olympians yelled good-bye to one another.

Then the boys ran north toward Olympia, hoping to steal the flame. And the girls ran south, hoping to find the torch.

CHAPTER THREE

A Trio of Monsters

It was mega-hot as the boys made their way north, following Chip's arrow. They tromped down dusty roads and across barren and rocky hills. Everyone they saw was heading in the opposite direction. Away from Olympia.

The boys had just caught sight of a mountain, when more fireballs blasted from the sky. But this time was different. The fireballs didn't explode when they hit the ground.

Instead they rolled up the road. Right toward the Olympians!

Poseidon's eyes bugged out. "Now Hyperion's *bowling* his fireballs?"

"Yeah. And we're the pins!" Hades exclaimed.

"Take cover!" yelled Zeus.

The boys dodged the balls and ran behind some rocks. So did several other travelers, including a young man with a beard.

Like most people they'd passed, he was carrying a big bundle on his back. Everyone was leaving the hot, dry places where they lived. They hoped to find cooler lands farther away, with water where they could farm and grow gardens again.

"Are you from Olympia?" Zeus asked the bearded man. "We heard Hyperion was there. We're looking for him."

Boom!

Just then the fireballs that had chased them exploded a ways down the road. An old woman sitting nearby let out a dry cackle of laughter. "You got a death wish or something?"

"Um, no," Poseidon said, looking alarmed, and a little bit chicken.

"Then if I were you, I'd turn around right now. Go back the way you came," the bearded man told them. "Fireballs are one thing. You can dodge those. But Hyperion's mere touch could fry you to a cinder! Nothing good can come from seeking him out."

Zeus gulped. "We have to see him, though," he said bravely. "We're on a quest."

Another fireball came crashing up the road. A gray-haired man dove in next to them, narrowly escaping being mowed down by it.

"Did you say 'quest'?" he asked, arching an eyebrow at Zeus. "Who sent you?"

"The Oracle at Delphi," Hades told him.

The old man gave a low laugh. "Pythia? I consulted her once. About buying some pigs. Instead she gave me some crazy advice about planting *figs*."

Zeus nodded. "She makes mistakes like that sometimes."

The old man grinned, as if remembering. "Worked out pretty well, though. I had years of excellent fig crops—till Hyperion came."

As the fireballs continued to rain down, the group stayed hidden. They shared what little food and drink they had. And they tried to sleep. At sunset the fireballs abruptly stopped. Just like they had the night before.

Once the moon rose, the boys crept out onto the road. Everyone else did too, all going their separate ways.

"Word to the wise," the gray-haired man

called to the Olympians. "Beware of the three creatures that guard the entrance to the temple Hyperion is using as his stronghold. Heard they're a dangerous lot."

"Thanks for the warning," Zeus called back.

As the three boys moved on, Chip's arrow glowed green, helping to light their way. It was pointing toward the mountain up ahead. Chip's map labeled it MOUNT CRONUS.

But when they reached the base of the mountain, there was a sign there that read: MOUNT KRONOS. The Titan king liked naming things after himself. But he was a horrible speller. Sometimes he even spelled his own name with a *K* instead of a *C* and substituted an *O* for a *U*.

"Stealing that flame won't be easy, you know," said Poseidon. As they began climbing, he was sounding more and more nervous. "I mean, Hyperion won't just *give* it to us."

"I know," Zeus said. "Don't worry. We'll figure something out."

"Think the dangerous creatures that guy told us about are more Creatures of Chaos?" Hades asked.

He was sounding jittery now too. And with good reason. King Cronus was always unleashing evil creatures on the world. It was like he was hoping to scare everyone into submission.

"Probably. But we can take them," Zeus said with more confidence than he felt. He figured it was a leader's job to encourage others.

"We've already done battle with a huge army of Androphagoi," he added. "What could be worse than monsters with sharp-toothed mouths smack dab in the middle of their chests?"

"Those punishment-obsessed Furies we met in the Underworld were pretty harsh too," said Poseidon.

"Right," said Zeus. "So compared to them, how bad could these three new monsters be?"

His companions paled. "Monsters?" echoed Poseidon.

"Oops. 'Creatures,' I meant," said Zeus. "Besides, don't forget we've got help. A trident, a helm, and this." He gave his thunderbolt a pat.

Hiking up the mountain was easier than it could have been. Because of the drought, there was no snow. Still, it took hours for the boys to reach the top. Once there they could see the city of Olympia in the valley down below.

"Look! The temple!" said Hades, pointing. Though it was still dark, Zeus was able to make out Doric columns. They surrounded the rectangular structure. Moonlight glinted off the roof's thin marble tiles.

As the boys set off for Olympia, they kept a lookout for the trio of dangerous monsters—uh, creatures. But all was quiet. By the time they reached the foothills, dawn was breaking.

They headed for the temple. They were almost to its steps when something swooped down from the sky to land before them. Its front half was a horse, but its back half was a winged rooster.

Hades made a sound that was part giggle and part gasp. "What is *that*?"

Was this one of the three creatures? wondered Zeus. If so, it didn't look all that scary.

"'Scuse me," said Zeus. "You're in our way." He started to go around the creature, but it moved to block him.

The creature stamped the ground with its two front horse hooves. It tossed its mane. "Neigh-a-doodle-do!" it said.

"Does that mean 'no'?" Poseidon asked it.

The creature scratched at the ground with its rooster claws, shook its rooster tail, and flapped

its yellow-feathered wings. "Cock-a-doodle-neigh!" it crowed.

The boys stared. Then they all started to laugh. They couldn't help it. This was the goofiest-looking creature they'd ever seen!

"Ha-ha-ha! What in the world are you?" Hades asked it. "A roosterdoodle?"

"Hee-hee. Or maybe a hooferdoodle? Or a wing-a-ling?" Poseidon asked.

The creature fixed them with an icy stare. Then it half-trotted and half-strutted toward them. "Whoodle doodle do you think you are?" it said in an annoyed voice. "If you think I look funny, have you tried looking in a mirror?"

"Whoa!" said Zeus. This caused the creature to come to an immediate halt. It acted as if there were reins around its horse head and Zeus had given them a yank.

"You can talk," Zeus said in amazement.

The odd-looking creature let out a sound that was half horse snort and half rooster squawk. "Of course I can. I'm a Hippalectryon, not a dodo bird."

"Hippa-what?" said Poseidon. He grinned at his companions. "Try saying *that* name three times fast!"

The boys began giggling again. The only way this monstrous creature was going to harm them was by making them laugh to death, thought Zeus. But their laughter was cut short when the Hippalectryon called for backup.

"Manticore! Onocentaur!" it whinny-crowed. Immediately two more creatures burst from around the sides of the temple. They stood on either side of the Hippalectryon, looking fierce.

The Onocentaur was similar to a centaur. Only instead of being half man and half horse, it was half man and half *donkey.* The Manticore

was scarier. It had the body of a lion, the tail of a scorpion, and the head of a man.

"State your business!" the Manticore ordered the boys. It had three rows of nasty-looking shark-like teeth inside its mouth. And it looked hungry.

Zeus considered those teeth. He also studied the sharp, pointy spines on the creature's tail. Were they poisonous? Just in case, he decided it might be best not to mess around.

"We're here to see Hyperion," he said in what he hoped was a commanding voice.

The creatures folded their wings, arms, and paws. They stared at the boys haughtily.

"And what makes you think that the High One, Lord of Light, Hyperion will want to see three little nothings like you!" brayed the Onocentaur.

"He's searching for a certain torch, isn't he?" Zeus said with a burst of inspiration.

The eyes of all three creatures went wide. In an instant they surrounded the Olympians. Suddenly they looked far more menacing. The boys didn't feel like laughing now.

"Doodle-do you have it?" the Hippalectryon demanded.

"I didn't say that," Zeus replied. He glanced at Poseidon and Hades. They nodded to show that they understood he was trying to trick their way into the temple. "But we might just have some information that—"

"Tell us what you know!" the Manticore interrupted. Its scorpion tail rattled menacingly. "Or else!"

"Oh, Manticore, give it a rest," said the Onocentaur. "Hyperion won't be happy if we slay them *before* he finds out the location of the torch."

"No, guess not," the Manticore said, sounding disappointed. "But maybe just one of them?"

"No! Now move it, boys," the Onocentaur instructed the Olympians.

"Unless you doodle-*do* want to become Manticore's breakfast," prodded the Hippalectryon.

And with that, the monstrous creatures ushered the three boys up the temple steps.

CHAPTER FOUR

The High One

Zeus, Hades, and Poseidon soon found themselves inside an enormous room within the temple. In the center of it was a huge marble statue of King Cronus seated astride a rearing horse.

"Wait here," the Onocentaur instructed them. Then he and his two companions disappeared into another part of the temple.

"Let's get out of here!" wailed Poseidon the minute the three boys were alone.

"No!" said Zeus. "We have to see Hyperion, remember? And somehow trick him into revealing the location of the flame so we can steal it."

"Zeus is right," Hades agreed.

To pass the time the boys began circling the statue that dominated the room, studying it. It nearly reached the ceiling of the huge temple. And it was so well sculpted that it almost appeared to be alive.

Poseidon pointed his trident at the statue's open mouth. "Cronus looks like he's shouting commands."

"To his army of Cronies, no doubt," said Zeus.

"Yeah, probably saying, 'Death to the Olympians!'" Hades shuddered.

Zeus eyed Poseidon's trident. "We'd better keep our magical objects hidden. So Hyperion won't try to take them."

"Good idea," said Poseidon. "Short!" he commanded the trident. Instantly it shrank down to only a foot and a half long. He tucked it under his belt, then arranged the folds of his tunic to cover it.

Worried that Bolt's occasional sparking might draw attention, Zeus removed it from its place at his side. After setting Bolt on the temple floor, he took off his belt, then retied it around his waist under his tunic.

Finally he tucked the bolt under his belt again so the tunic covered both belt and bolt. No way Hyperion would spot it now. At least Zeus hoped not.

"What should I do with my helm?" asked Hades. "It doesn't get any smaller."

Zeus rolled his eyes. "Do I have to think of everything? Put it on. Then it and you will *both* be hidden."

"Awesome idea!" said Hades. Two seconds later he and his helm went invisible.

Just in the nick of time too. Because a giant strode into the room right then. He was as tall as the statue of Cronus! And his entire head glowed like a pale sun.

"Hyperion!" Zeus whispered to his companions, recognizing the Titan instantly.

That night in the forest, when Zeus had thrown his thunderbolt down the king's throat, this Titan had saved Cronus from choking. And that's when the king had barfed up the five Olympians imprisoned in his belly.

Hyperion's eyebrows rose when he saw Zeus. "Good to see you again," he said. Then he smiled warmly. A little *too* warmly.

As the room heated up, Zeus began to sweat. Suddenly he wished he could take off his tunic. And jump into a lake. One that was full of ice.

In his mind Zeus quickly ran over the plan the boys had discussed earlier. It went like this:

Step one: Trick Hyperion.

Step two: Find the flame.

Step three: Escape with it.

Only now it struck him that the plan might've benefitted from a few more in-between steps. And some details about how to accomplish those things.

Hyperion switched his solar-heated gaze to Poseidon. "Well, if it isn't one of the barf boys," he taunted. "Looks like you managed to clean yourself up a little since the last time I saw you."

Luckily, Hyperion didn't seem to know that there were supposed to be *three* boys in the room. His goofy creature-guards must not have mentioned that fact.

Hyperion snapped his fingers. A golden throne magically appeared in front of the statue. He sat in it and got down to his evil business. "My guards say you have information about a certain . . . *object* . . . I've been searching for."

Zeus gulped. He racked his brain, trying to think of some way to trick Hyperion into telling them where he kept the flame. But before Zeus could get any great ideas, the Titan spoke again.

"But where are my manners? You boys look tired and hot. Lemonade, anyone?" Hyperion snapped his fingers again. This time a pitcher magically appeared.

Zeus and Poseidon eyed it thirstily and nodded.

Hyperion took a long gulp straight from the pitcher. "Ahhh," he said. "Delicious!"

The boys leaned forward. They licked their lips.

"Your turn," Hyperion said. He reached out as if to hand the pitcher to Zeus. Then he deliberately let it drop to the floor. *Thunk!*

"Oops, clumsy me," he said, laughing as the pitcher fell over on its side. Made of thick ceramic, it didn't break.

Before the lemonade could spill out and spread over the floor's mosaic tiles, Poseidon made a grab for his trident. "Long!" he shouted.

Zeus watched in horror as the golden trident lengthened. Seemingly unaware of what he'd revealed, Poseidon used his trident to suck up the lemonade. Then he drank thirstily as lemonade sprayed from the trident's middle prong like a fountain.

"It's good," he told Zeus. "Want some?"

Zeus groaned.

Hyperion slowly rose to his feet, his eyes gleaming. "That's Oceanus's trident!" he exclaimed. Oceanus was another Titan buddy of his and the king's. The boys had tangled with him on an earlier quest to a boiling sea.

Poseidon blinked, realizing his mistake. "No, it's mine," he countered, clutching the trident with both hands. "Oceanus stole it from me, but—"

"Well, it's *mine* now!" exclaimed Hyperion. Sparks and cinders flew from him as he reached toward Poseidon. At his fiery touch the golden trident glowed red-hot.

"Ow!" shouted Poseidon. He dropped the trident like a hot potato. It clanked to the floor as he blew on the palms of his hands to cool them.

Zeus lunged for the trident. But Hyperion moved faster. He picked up the trident, which looked the size of a fork in his big hands. The instant he grabbed it, it enlarged dramatically. It was now three times as long as Poseidon was tall!

"This will make a nice addition to the magical object collection I'm putting together for King Cronus," Hyperion said. His eyes burned into Zeus's. "Got anything else for me? Like that thunderbolt you had last time we met, perhaps?"

"Nope. I, um, lost it," Zeus lied. He could feel it under his tunic and just hoped Hyperion didn't have solar X-ray vision.

"Oh, too bad," said the Titan. He gave a low, evil laugh.

Zeus wasn't sure if Hyperion really believed him. Maybe he was just biding his time. Maybe he thought that if Zeus *did* have the thunderbolt, he'd get it off him later.

Regardless, Zeus was having second thoughts about using Bolt to fight the sun-headed Titan.

Hyperion's fiery touch hadn't melted the trident. But if his power clashed with the thunderbolt's electric charge, who knew what might happen?

"King Cronus will be quite pleased I've captured this trident for him," Hyperion said. With a snap of his fingers, a table magically appeared next to his throne. He set the trident on top of it. Then he plopped onto his throne again. "He was none too happy when Oceanus lost it."

"He didn't *lose* it," Poseidon argued. "I *took* it from him."

Zeus jumped when he felt a light tap on his shoulder. Hades whispered in his ear. "As soon as the trident cools down, I'll grab it off the table."

"Good plan," Zeus said.

"What's a good plan?" Hyperion asked. Apparently Zeus had spoken louder than he'd intended.

Zeus thought fast. "Um . . . your plan to collect magical objects for King Cronus. I'm sure he'll be grateful. Maybe he'll even make you his second in command."

Hyperion frowned. "I already am."

"Oh," said Zeus. Here was his chance to find out about the flame. "How amazing! You must be really good at getting things done. So, how many magical objects have you already collected?" he asked in a fake admiring tone.

"Besides the trident?" Hyperion replied proudly. "Just one so far."

"More like one half, actually." said Poseidon, sounding angry. "A flame without a torch, right?"

Hyperion leaned forward. His blazing eyes narrowed. "What would you know about that?"

"Nothing," Zeus said quickly. "Some villagers mentioned it. Said you need a certain torch to make it work?"

As he spoke, he noticed the trident move slightly. Hades must be over by the table trying to pick it up.

Hyperion smirked at Zeus. "And I suppose you know where that *certain torch* can be found?"

"Maybe," Zeus said. He had to keep Hyperion talking so he wouldn't notice the trident wiggling. "If I could get a look at the flame, I might be able to tell you if the torch I know about is the one you need."

"Uh-huh. Sure," Hyperion said sarcastically. "Pull the other leg." Looking skeptical, he started to stand.

Just then the trident rolled off the table. *Bam!* "Ow! Ow!" Hyperion yelled. The trident had hit his toe. He hopped around in pain, then bent and grabbed one end of the trident.

It jerked, trying to get away from him. "What the—," he said in surprise. He pulled it closer. It jerked away again. It was a trident tug-of-war!

Hyperion eyed Zeus and Poseidon suspiciously. "I don't know how you're making it move, but you're not getting it back."

Yanking hard on the trident, he managed to take it from the invisible Hades. He lifted it in his fist and then shook it in triumph at the two Olympians he could see.

"This trident is mine now. As are you. King Cronus will be very pleased at your capture." Glancing over his shoulder, Hyperion called out, "Guards! Come take them away!"

"Run!" shouted Zeus. He and Poseidon made a dash for the door. Too late. The three oddball creatures who'd brought them inside were blocking the exit.

"Call off the guards!" yelled a voice. It was Hades!

A look of confusion stole over Hyperion's face. "Who said that?" He glanced around the room. "Show yourself!"

CHAPTER FIVE

Lightning Strikes Twice

"Call off the guards," Hades repeated. He was still invisible.

"What magic is this?" Hyperion demanded, looking a little nervous.

He motioned for the guards to draw back. The Hippalectryon, Onocentaur, and Manticore moved away from the boys. But they continued to stand at the ready. Their wings, arms, and paws were flexed at their sides.

Hyperion's glowing eyes swept the room. "I did what you asked. Now show yourself, whoever you are."

"First you must return the trident to Poseidon," Hades ordered. Since the last quest, when he'd found out he was lord of the Underworld, he'd become quite bold. Especially when he was invisible.

"Oh, all right," muttered Hyperion. With an annoyed expression he tossed the trident back to Poseidon.

The minute Poseidon touched it, it shrank back to a size he could handle. But that didn't mean he *should* handle it right then. Because it was still hot.

"Yeowch!" yelled Poseidon. He tossed the trident from hand to hand as he waited for it to cool.

Meanwhile Hades removed the helm and became visible. He was standing right beside Hyperion's throne.

"The Helm of Darkness!" Hyperion exclaimed. His hands twitched as he stared at the glittering jeweled crown Hades held. "I thought it was hidden in the Underworld."

"It was," said Hades. "I found it there. Now it's mine." He stuck out his chest proudly. "Because I'm lord of the Underworld."

"Underworld, Schmunderworld," Hyperion scoffed. Without warning he made a lunge for the jeweled helm. "Give me that thing!"

"No! Toss it here!" Zeus called out to Hades.

Wasting no time, Hades pitched the crown toward him.

Zeus raised his arms to catch it. But as the helm sailed his way, the Manticore swung its scorpion tail high. The tail snagged the helm in midair!

"Thief! Give it back!" Hades commanded.

Poseidon thrust out his now cool trident. He

tried to use it to hook the helm off the Manticore's tail. But the Manticore flipped the helm to the Onocentaur, and then wrapped its tail around the trident. It yanked. Hard.

The trident slipped from Poseidon's hands. Now the Manticore had it!

The Onocentaur brayed with laughter. The half man, half donkey set the helm on top of its head. "How do I look?" it asked its friends.

"Better than ever," the Manticore replied. "Because I can't see your ugly mug anymore."

The Hippalectryon flapped its wings and grinned. "Or the rest of youdle-doodle either."

"Stop goofing around, idiots! Hand those things to me this instant!" roared Hyperion.

The Onocentaur reappeared at once. Then it and the Manticore sheepishly handed over the helm and the trident. Both objects enlarged and glowed red in Hyperion's hands.

"Including these I now have *three* magical objects," he gloated.

"Well, two and a half, anyway," Zeus corrected.

"Whatever." Hyperion hooked his thumb toward the enormous statue behind him. "As I said before, King Cronus will be very glad to see them. And you three as well."

"Get them!" he ordered the guards.

"Do something!" Hades hissed at Zeus.

Left no other choice, Zeus whipped the thunderbolt dagger out from under his tunic and belt.

"Large!" he commanded. A sound like the cracking of a glacier rang through the room. Sparking with electricity, Bolt expanded to its full length of five feet.

Zeus stared Hyperion down. "Return the trident and helm!" Holding the thunderbolt, he drew back his arm. He was poised to hurl the bolt right at the fiery Titan.

"Looks like your lost thunderbolt just turned up," Hyperion said sarcastically.

Before Zeus could reply, Bolt was smacked from his hand. *Whap!*

"Yow!" the Onocentaur yelped as the bolt spiraled up into the air. The creature had kicked out with its donkey hind legs and knocked the thunderbolt away! But its legs had received quite a nasty electric shock in the process.

As luck would have it, Bolt went whirling up toward King Cronus's statue. *Thunk!* The thunderbolt stuck point-first in the marble king's open mouth. It lost its sizzle and glow the minute it lodged in the statue.

"Well, well, well," Hyperion said, chortling. "And they say lightning doesn't strike twice in the same place. King Cronus—the real one—

wasn't too happy when your thunderbolt went down his throat the first time. You escaped punishment then. But this time you won't be so lucky."

Turning his back to the boys and the guards, Hyperion stepped up to the statue. His eyes glowed as he reached for the bolt. "Now I'll have this magical object to add to my collection too! And once I have the torch, I'll deliver everything to King Cronus."

Hyperion gave the bolt a tug. Nothing happened. He tried again, tugging harder. But still the thunderbolt stayed stubbornly stuck.

"What's the matter, Your Brilliance?" taunted Zeus. "Not strong enough for the job?"

Hyperion pulled as hard as he could, muscles bulging. Still the bolt didn't budge. Because there was something "The High One" didn't know that Zeus did. Bolt couldn't be freed from stone—any kind of stone—without Zeus's help.

"Maybe you need to start doing push-ups," Poseidon chimed in.

"Better watch it or you'll soon be too weak to throw your fireballs," Hades teased.

Hyperion whirled toward them. His eyes went flat and hard. "Take them to the globe of destruction!" he ordered the guards.

The creature-guards surrounded the three Olympians again. "Don't even think about trying to make a run for it," the Manticore warned them. It gave its scorpion tail a rattle.

Zeus glared at Hyperion. "Let us go, you . . . you, glowworm! You can't keep us here. We're Olympians!"

"Olympians, Schmolympians," Hyperion sneered. "You're all a bit on the scrawny side for my taste, but Olympians are the king's favorite snack. As you well know. Take them away!" he ordered the guards.

Immediately the boys were rounded up and marched out of the room. "Down the stairs!" ordered the Manticore when they came to a set of steps. The boys stumbled down them as the three creature-guards followed behind.

The bottom of the steps opened up into another room underground. The boys' eyes widened when they saw what was inside: a huge flaming globe. It was about three times as tall as they were.

Zeus gulped. This had to be the globe of destruction Hyperion had mentioned.

With its back to the globe, the Onocentaur kicked at it three times with one of its hooves. *Kick! Kick! Kick!* A door appeared. The globe was hollow inside!

"In you go!" said the half man, half donkey.

Wings, arms, and paws herded the three boys inside. The fiery door slid shut behind them. The guards stomped away up the stairs again.

The boys were trapped. In a fiery prison!

CHAPTER SIX

Global Warming

Zeus slipped off a sandal. *Thwack! Thwack!* He hit at the place where the globe had opened. But nothing happened. Except that his sandal began to smoke from the heat. At least the floor under their feet wasn't fiery. Only the walls of the globe were.

"It's as hot as the Underworld in here," Poseidon complained.

"Seems just right to me," said Hades. "Nice

and toasty." Cold bothered him, but heat never did. "And anyway, we wouldn't be here if you hadn't lost your trident to Hyperion. *Twice.*"

"I was thirsty," Poseidon whined. "Besides, this is just as much your fault as mine. Why did you have to play the hero and take off your helm?"

Hades frowned. "Duh. To keep those guards from taking you and Zeus away."

"But if you'd stayed invisible, you could've followed when the guards brought us down here," Poseidon argued. "Then, when they left, you could've opened the door of this globe from the outside and—"

"We all made mistakes," Zeus interrupted. "I was dumb not to keep my thunderbolt hidden. Now none of us has a weapon!"

Pythia's prophecy said Zeus was the leader of the Olympians. But sometimes he doubted himself when he made mistakes like that. Did he truly have what it took to be a good leader? he wondered.

"What's done is done," he told his companions. "Arguing won't help. The thing now is to think of an escape plan."

"You're right," said Hades.

Poseidon nodded.

The three boys began pacing circles inside the flaming globe while trying to think up a plan.

"Maybe we could run from one side to the other superfast and *ram* through the globe door," Poseidon suggested.

Hades snorted. "Okay. You can be the first to try it. Zeus and I will scoop up your ashes afterward."

"You got a better idea?" Poseidon said with a scowl.

"Not yet," said Hades. "But *any* idea would be better than yours."

"I know!" said Zeus. Poseidon and Hades stopped arguing and turned to look at him. "The guards will return with food and drink eventually. After all, Hyperion needs to keep us alive."

"True," said Hades. "Till he can turn us over to the king."

"And so?" Poseidon asked.

Zeus grinned. "So when the guards open the globe, we'll trick them somehow and escape!" Abruptly his grin evaporated. "I haven't quite yet worked out the *somehow* part," he admitted.

Just then a tiny voice piped up. "Et-lip e-mip elp-hip."

"Chip?" Zeus had almost forgotten about the amulet. It didn't speak often, but when it did, it spoke Chip Latin. Which was like Pig Latin. Except that you moved the first letter of a word to the end of it and then added an *ip* sound, as in "chip."

Zeus lifted the amulet from around his neck. "Did you just say 'Let me help?'" he asked it.

"Es-yip," said Chip.

Poseidon and Hades came closer. The three Olympians gazed at the amulet with hope in their eyes.

"How can you help?" Zeus asked. "Do you have a plan? 'Cause we could really use one."

"E-bip ilent-sip," Chip said.

"Be silent?" Zeus glanced up at Hades and Poseidon. He put his finger to his lips. "Shh," Zeus whispered. "Chip needs quiet time to think of a plan."

"O-nip!" squeaked Chip. "Ilence-sip is-ip e-thip an-plip."

"'Silence is the plan,'" translated Hades. "What's that supposed to mean?"

Zeus thought for a minute. Finally he snapped his fingers. "I think Chip wants us to be quiet when the guards come back!" He stared at the amulet. "Right, Chip? Is that what you want us to do?"

"Ight-rip," said Chip.

"And then what?" asked Poseidon. "What's the rest of the plan?"

But now Chip clammed up and wouldn't say.

"Maybe Chip doesn't know the rest of the plan," said Zeus. He slipped the amulet back inside the neck of his tunic. "Maybe we'll just have to wing it when the time comes."

"We *winged* it before," Hades said glumly. "That's how we wound up here."

"Yeah, I know," said Zeus. "But—"

"Shh!" hissed Poseidon. "I hear something."

Sure enough they could hear hooves trotting down the stairs. The Onocentaur, Zeus guessed. Good. One guard would be much easier to deal with than all three.

"Lunchtime!" brayed the Onocentaur. Seconds

later the door to the globe slid partway open. The half man, half donkey tossed a leather water pouch inside. Poseidon caught it before it could hit the floor.

With one swift motion he pulled out the cork plug. He tipped the pouch toward him and drank, then passed it to the others.

The Onocentaur laughed. "Heat making you thirsty, huh?" The creature pulled a loaf of bread and a big chunk of cheese from a bag slung over its shoulder. It tossed those in too.

Hades caught the bread. Zeus caught the cheese. Holding on to the food, they stared at the Onocentaur but said nothing.

"Well? Aren't you going to say 'thank you'?" it demanded.

All three boys kept stubbornly silent. Suddenly Chip piped up. "Ank-thip ou-yip," it said in its squeaky little voice.

"Huh?" The Onocentaur looked from one boy to the other. "Who said that?"

The boys didn't reply. Their lips were zipped.

But Chip's weren't. "Ust-jip e-mip," it said.

The creature scowled at the boys. "I was watching all of you. How come no one's lips moved?"

The Onocentaur kicked at the fiery door with one of its hooves, opening it wider. It took a step inside the globe. "Is someone else in here, hiding behind you?" It tried to peer around the boys.

Staying silent, they scooted closer together, standing all in a row. The Onocentaur got even more suspicious. It rushed to the boys and pushed behind them to look for the source of the squeaky voice.

Catching Poseidon's and Hades' eyes, Zeus nodded toward the door. The creature was behind them and the door was open in front of them. This was their chance to escape!

Without a word the three boys leaped from the globe faster than even Zeus's thunderbolt could have flashed. The minute they were out, Zeus threw the hunk of cheese at the fiery door. It slammed shut, trapping the Onocentaur inside.

Bam! Bam! The creature brayed and kicked at the door, but to no avail.

"Yes! Trapped!" yelled Poseidon. "See how you like it in there, Your Donkeyship."

The heat from the door had melted the cheese. Before it could glop onto the floor, Hades reached toward it with the bread loaf. The cheese fell on top.

"Mmm, toasted cheese sandwich," he said, taking a bite. He broke off cheesy chunks and handed them to the others.

"Let's go!" Zeus called over his shoulder as he made for the stairs. Only it sounded more like, "Mesh gor," since his mouth was full of food.

Hades and Poseidon understood, though. They followed right on his heels.

Hyperion was nowhere in sight as the boys entered the upstairs room.

"Where do you think he is?" Hades whispered.

Poseidon pointed toward a window. "Sun's high. So he's probably off throwing fireballs at unlucky villagers. What I want to know is, where's my trident?"

While Poseidon and Hades began looking around for their stolen magical objects, Zeus ran to the gigantic statue. Quickly he shimmied up it.

Once he reached the top, he plucked his thunderbolt from the marble King Cronus's open mouth, as easy as pulling a knife from butter. Just in time too.

"You there! Halt!" The Manticore and the

Hippalectryon padded and trot-strutted into the room to confront them.

Zing! Zing! From his perch on the statue, Zeus whipped his five-foot-long thunderbolt back and forth in great swishes at them. They turned pale at the sight of the sizzling, sparking thunderbolt.

"He pulled it out!" cried the Manticore.

"Not even the great Hyperion was able to doodle-do that!" said the Hippalectryon. "We must inform him." With that, the two creatures turned tail and ran out of the room.

"Go get 'em, Bolt!" Zeus commanded. He released the thunderbolt. Happy to be free again, Bolt chased after the guards. Zeus scrambled down from the statue.

"Ow! Ouch! Yikes!" Zeus could hear the creatures yelling as his thunderbolt chased them, zapping them with glee.

CHAPTER SEVEN

Theia

"I bet my trident's in here," said Poseidon. He thumped on a humongous wooden chest sitting in a corner of the room.

Well, it looked humongous to the Olympians, anyway. To Hyperion it probably looked the size of a jewelry box, thought Zeus. And maybe that's what it was. Or maybe it held the flame! Unfortunately, it was locked.

Getting an idea, Zeus whistled toward the

doorway. "Bolt! Come back, boy!" he called out. A few seconds later the thunderbolt zipped back to him.

"Can you cut through this lock?" Zeus asked the bolt.

Bolt reared back as if doubtful. Then, ignoring the lock, it sliced the top off the wooden chest instead.

After a stunned moment Hades said, "Good thinking, Bolt!"

Sparking with pride, the thunderbolt hovered nearby, waiting. Together the boys heaved the chest's sliced-off lid onto the floor.

When Hades and Zeus boosted Poseidon up to look inside, he gave a whoop. "Yes! I was right! The trident and helm are in there. Nothing else, though."

"I was kind of hoping the flame might be in there too," Zeus said. "But I guess that wouldn't make sense. It would burn right through wood."

Pounding footsteps alerted the boys that the two guards were coming back. And it sounded like the Onocentaur was with them! The boys could hear him braying in anger.

Using Bolt, Zeus thunder-pole-vaulted into the chest. He tossed out the trident and helm, and the other two boys caught them. Then he thunder-pole-vaulted back out.

The minute the boys ran outside, a fireball landed in their path. *Boom! Sssst!*

Zeus glanced up. He pointed. "It's Hyperion! He's on the roof of the temple!"

"Prepare to be toast! You'll never escape me!" yelled the sun-headed Titan. He wound up and pitched another fireball their way.

Boom! Sssst! This one exploded too close for comfort.

Despite their magic the bolt, trident, and

helm were no match for exploding fireballs. "Run!" Zeus yelled.

The boys ran. But the three creature-guards were also outside now. And they were blocking the way back up the mountain. The boys screeched to a halt.

They turned and ran the opposite direction. It wasn't the way they needed to go to meet up with Hera and Demeter again. But at least they'd be able to avoid the guards. And have less chance of being blown to smithereens!

Fireballs rained down on them as they fled. They darted from rock to rock and bush to bush to stay hidden. Finally, after several more hours, night fell and the fireballs stopped.

The boys wandered aimlessly through the forested foothills with only the moon to guide them. They grew tired and hungry and, eventually, lost.

"We failed," said Hades.

"Don't rub it in," said Poseidon.

"We'll try again. Don't worry. The magical flame will soon be ours," Zeus said. But this time it was hard to sound encouraging. He was losing hope himself.

"Hey! There's a light up ahead," Hades announced after a bit.

A flicker of hope rose in Zeus again. "Maybe it's the flame!"

They stumbled toward it. "No! It's a house!" said Poseidon as they drew near.

"Careful. This house is too big for mortals. Giants probably live here," said Zeus.

Still, the delicious smell of fresh-baked bread drew the hungry boys on, despite the danger. They stashed their magical objects behind a woodpile at the side of the house, then headed for the door.

Just as they reached it, the door flew open. A woman with a stiff, puffy hairstyle stood before them. Her brown eyes were heavily made up. And she was supertall. Titan tall.

Uh-oh, thought Zeus.

"Thought I heard the pitter-patter of little feet," she told them. "Come in. I've been expecting you!" Her unnaturally long, thick eyelashes gave a flutter.

Zeus blinked in surprise. "You have?" How had she known they were coming? Was this Titan an oracle, like Pythia? She didn't *look* like one. Pythia dressed in a plain hooded robe and had shiny black hair that hung to her knees.

"Of course," the woman said. "My husband promised to send me some servants." She pursed her painted red lips. "Only I didn't expect you to be so young. Or so small. But I suppose you'll have to do."

The woman's glittering golden gown rustled softly as she moved aside for the boys to enter. She adjusted her feather boa.

Poseidon crossed his arms, frowning. "We're not ser—"

"We're stronger than we look," interrupted Zeus.

He glanced meaningfully at Poseidon and Hades. He hoped they'd realize he wanted them to play along. It wasn't safe to reveal their true identities. Not yet, anyway. Not before they got some food and found out who this Titan lady was. Maybe never!

"Good," said the woman. She led the boys to her kitchen, where a small fire blazed in the hearth.

"My name's Theia," she said. "And your names are . . . ?"

"Goose," said Zeus.

Poseidon and Hades giggled.

Zeus turned red. In his haste to hide his true identity, the nickname had been the first thing to pop into his head. He wished he could take it back. But now it was too late.

Theia arched an eyebrow at him. "Your name's 'Goose'?" she said, sounding amused. "Your mother must've been feeling hungry when she named you that." She threw back her head and laughed.

"Yes, ma'am. I suppose she was," Zeus said. He pointed to Poseidon and Hades, who were both still smirking at him. It was time for a little payback, he decided. "And these are my friends, Fishbreath and Stinkboy," he announced.

The two boys scowled at him. Now it was Zeus's turn to grin.

Theia laughed harder still. "That's some sense of humor your parents have."

"Yeah," Hades said drily. "They were probably a couple of crack-ups."

"Probably? Oh, I'm sorry," Theia said gently. "Are you orphans, then?"

Immediately Poseidon pressed his hands over his heart, playing on her sympathy. "Yes. We are," he said with downcast eyes.

Good one, thought Zeus. Though in truth he didn't know anything about the other Olympians' parents. It was something they'd never discussed.

Theia clucked. "You poor things," she said. "It was nice of my husband to take you in and give you jobs, then." She gave her head a slight shake. "He does have a good side. It's King Cronus who's a bad influence on him."

The three Olympians darted nervous looks at one another. Zeus wanted to ask who Theia's husband was. But if he did, she'd know the boys were imposters—that her husband hadn't really sent them.

He gulped as a new thought came to him. What if the *real* servants arrived while the boys were still there? He hoped they wouldn't come until morning. By then maybe the boys would be fed and rested. And long gone.

He couldn't help glancing at the gigantic loaves of bread cooling on top of a table. *Mmm.* They smelled so good. He must've drooled a little, because Theia smiled at him.

"Hungry?" she asked.

All three boys nodded.

"Then help me get dinner ready," she said, putting them to work.

Poseidon started peeling potatoes the size of pumpkins for stew. And Hades struggled to wield a knife as long as a sword to chop carrots as thick as his arms.

Theia sent Zeus out to chop wood. The ax was way too big and heavy for him to handle. After checking to see that no one was around, he whistled softly for Bolt. "Come, boy. I need your help!"

On command Bolt zipped from behind the woodpile, all aglow.

"Okay. Let's get to work," said Zeus. He swung the thunderbolt at a thick chunk of firewood.

Crack! The wood split right down the middle.

"Good job!" Zeus said softly. At the praise, Bolt glowed even more brightly. Before long they'd chopped a nice stack of wood. It was a bit charred around the edges, though. He hoped Theia wouldn't notice.

As the thunderbolt hid again, Zeus took a load of wood into the cottage. There he added it to the fire.

Theia had hung a big pot full of water and meat over the hearth. Now she added the potatoes and carrots that the other two boys had chopped.

Hades and Poseidon had begun to set the table. Poseidon lined up silverware. Hades carried bowls as big as sinks to the table.

"Should we set a place for your husband, too?" Hades asked.

Theia laughed lightly. "No need . . . uh . . . *Stinkboy*. He won't be home tonight. Sent word he'd lost something and had to work late tonight to find it again. Just set places for yourselves and for me. Oh! And a place for Hestia, too."

CHAPTER EIGHT

Something Fishy

"Hestia?" echoed Zeus.

Poseidon uttered a strangled cry.

Crash! Hades dropped the bowl he was holding. It shattered against the tiled floor. "Oops! Sorry!" he said.

"Not to worry," said Theia. She kept on stirring the stew with a big wooden spoon. "Accidents happen. Just finish setting the table. I'll sweep up the pieces later."

"Um, is Hestia your daughter?" Zeus asked. He tried to sound casual. After all, there could be other girls named Hestia besides the Olympian girl they sought.

Theia laughed. "No. My children are all grown up. Hestia is my husband's—that is, *Hyperion's*—niece."

Poseidon and Zeus looked at each other with wide eyes. Hades dropped another bowl. *Crash!*

Theia looked over at him. "Maybe I'd better assign you a different task. Before all of my bowls are broken?"

"Sorry," Hades said again. "Guess I'm just clumsy tonight." He shot Zeus a glance and began picking up the broken pieces.

"So where is Hestia?" asked Poseidon.

Theia pointed with her wooden spoon to a room across the hall. "She's taking a nap. Such a nice girl, but very quiet. Hasn't said a word since she came here a few weeks ago. It's almost like there's a spell on her tongue."

Zeus peered toward the door she'd pointed to. King Cronus had ordered Hyperion to capture Hestia, put a spell on her, and hide her here. He was sure of it!

Theia honestly didn't seem to know that Hestia wasn't Hyperion's niece, however. His spell must have been keeping Hestia from telling the truth of who she was.

Just then the door across the way opened. A girl stepped out of the room. Her light brown hair was tangled from sleep.

Her brown eyes lit on Zeus first. He smiled, but the look she returned was vacant. *Lights on. Nobody home,* he thought.

But that changed the moment Poseidon and

Hades called out to her. "Hestia!" they exclaimed in joyful voices.

Her head turned toward them. All at once her eyes widened and became bright. Whatever spell had been holding her speechless fell away at the sight of the two boys.

"Poseidon? Hades? I thought I'd never see you again!" she cried out. She flew to the boys and hugged them. "But where are Hera and Demeter?" she asked.

"They stayed behind," said Poseidon, casting a wary eye in Theia's direction. She was gazing at them with suspicion now.

"Well, who's that?" Hestia asked, staring at Zeus.

Theia was staring at him now too. "You're Zeus, aren't you!" she exclaimed suddenly. "And you're all Olympians! You tricked me."

Braced for the worst, the four Olympians began backing away.

Theia pointed her wooden spoon at them. "Stop right there."

"Or what?" challenged Zeus. He'd hoped she would have a good heart, but he should have known better.

"Or you'll miss dinner," she said.

The Olympians looked at one another in surprise.

Turned out Theia *did* have a good heart. And she wasn't as completely trusting of Hyperion as they'd feared.

Over bowls of the delicious stew and thick slices of warm bread, the boys took turns explaining about their quest. They told Theia and Hestia how Hyperion had been wreaking havoc with fireballs and drought. They even brought their magical objects inside the house to show them off.

"Hyperion has stolen the flame that lights the Olympic Torch. The torch that the oracle Pythia sent us to find. Did he tell you that?" Hades asked Theia.

"No." Theia's lips tightened. "I thought I smelled something fishy."

Poseidon stopped eating, looking alarmed. "Is it me?" He sniffed himself. "It's probably because I'm god of the sea. Sorry, I—"

Theia interrupted him. "No, that was just a figure of speech," she said kindly. "I meant that I already suspected Hyperion was up to something." She glanced at Poseidon again. "Of course, I'd be lying if I said you smell as sweet as a rose, but— Well, never mind."

She ladled more stew into Zeus's huge bowl. He was so hungry, he'd finished off the first bowl in record time. "I met your mother once, you know," she told him.

Zeus's jaw dropped. "You did?"

Theia glanced around the table, then nodded. "She was a wonderful woman. And absolutely determined to keep you safe from harm."

"Is that why she left me in that cave on Crete?" Zeus asked excitedly. He'd long wondered about his parents, hoping to find them someday. "Is—is she still alive?"

Theia nodded again. "She's alive. And probably with Cronus, but I—"

Zeus sucked in his breath, imagining his mother locked up in a castle tower. Or in the depths of a gloomy dungeon. He jumped up.

"Then I'll rescue her!" he said fiercely. "Where is she?"

Stomp! Stomp! Stomp!

Before he could ask any more questions, they heard the stamping of heavy feet outside.

Theia ran to peer out a window at the front of the house. "Half-giants. Cronus's soldiers," she told the others. "Quick! I'll delay them while you all duck out Hestia's bedroom window in the back."

"Why should we trust you?" asked Zeus. "You're a *Titan*. Hyperion's *wife*."

"Your mother was kind to me," Theia told him. After grabbing an unlit oil lamp, she ran to kneel before the hearth. "I owe her a big favor. And now I'm going to repay it."

With those words she poked a long, thin stick into the hearth fire. When the tip of the stick burst into flame, she used it to light the lamp. But oddly, the moment the flames in the hearth had leaped to the stick, the fire in the hearth had snuffed out. Only smoke remained to curl up the chimney.

Theia tried to hand the lamp to Zeus as everyone hurried into the bedroom. Clouds had moved in to hide the moon. It was pitch-black outside, Zeus realized. They would need light. But the flame in the lamp was dim now. And he was reluctant to take any gift from a Titan. Even a nice one.

"Take it," said Theia. "I'm almost certain it's the magic flame you seek."

At that, all four Olympians stopped in their tracks. Their eyes went to the lamp and they stared in amazement.

"The magic flame that lights the Olympic Torch!" Zeus exclaimed, catching on at last.

"It was here all along," said Poseidon.

"Hyperion hid it right in plain sight. In your hearth!" Hades added in a stunned voice.

Boom! Boom! Just then the soldiers pounded on the door.

"Yes. I'd seen him hide something there days ago, but didn't put two and two together until you mentioned the flame he'd stolen. Now take it and go," insisted Theia.

"Do as she says," Hestia urged. "She has been kind to me. I don't think she means us harm."

Oomph! Oomph! Hades and Poseidon leaped out the back window. As Hestia followed the boys out, Zeus took the lamp from Theia.

"I won't be able to help you after this," she warned him solemnly. "And I'll tell Hyperion you *stole* the flame."

"I understand." Clutching the lamp, Zeus ran for the window. "About my mother," he called back over his shoulder. "Where—"

But Theia had already gone to answer the

door. Frustrated at missing his chance to learn more, Zeus climbed outside. Then, with the lamp to light his way, he ran to catch up with the others.

CHAPTER NINE

The Journey Back

When Zeus caught up to his friends, he handed the lamp to Hades. Then he pulled up on the leather cord around his neck.

"I can't believe it! We got the flame!" Hades crowed.

"We are awesome!" said Poseidon. "Now let's just hope Hera and Demeter somehow managed to find the torch it's supposed to light."

Hestia smiled. "Ooh! I can hardly wait to see them again!"

The boys looked at Zeus, waiting for Chip's directions. Hestia stared at it curiously until Hades explained how it worked.

"That way," Zeus told the others after consulting the amulet. "Looks like we'll have to pass Hyperion's temple on the way."

"Not so awesome," said Poseidon.

But with no other choice the Olympians followed Chip's arrow. They stayed close together as they headed toward Hyperion's temple once again. The lamp's flame remained dim, but it helped light their way through the dark night.

Hestia had already heard much about their adventures at dinner. But as they traveled on, the boys filled her in on everything she'd missed while she'd been held captive.

"But why does the flame need to be contained

in a special torch?" she said after a while. "Why can't we just keep it in this lamp?"

"Well, the flame and the torch are both probably magic," mused Hades.

"I guess their magic gets super-charged when they're joined together," said Poseidon.

"But what does their combined magic do?" Hestia asked.

Poseidon shrugged. "Pythia didn't tell us."

"But it's bound to be something good," Zeus said. "Or she wouldn't have asked us to find it."

"It'll be something to help the villagers, I bet," said Hades. "Hyperion's fireballs have dried out the land. The drought has destroyed their crops. People are abandoning their homes."

"Then we must defeat him," Hestia said in a determined voice. "We must join the flame and torch together. And then we'll just see what happens!"

A few hours later the Olympians reached the valley. Hyperion's temple was dark and quiet. Giving it a wide berth, the four travelers crept on by. Then they continued up and over the mountain, to meet up with Hera and Demeter.

"That was surprisingly easy," Hades remarked.

Poseidon nodded. "Hera said Hyperion's sort of like the sun, right? So I think he must have to sleep at night. That's probably why the fireballs always come to a halt at sunset."

Zeus stopped to check Chip's arrow again. He handed the lamp off to the nearest person, who happened to be Hestia.

The minute she took it, Zeus noticed something interesting. The flame inside the lamp flared higher and glowed more brightly than ever before.

"Wow! That's better," said Poseidon.

"Yeah," agreed Hades. "Now we can actually see the path!"

As the Olympians moved on, Zeus thought about his mother. She was alive! Theia had said so. He could recall Theia's words exactly: *She was a wonderful woman. And absolutely determined to keep you safe from harm.*

But where was she now? Was she in danger? Had Cronus kept her prisoner all these years? Maybe because she'd refused to tell him where she'd hidden Zeus? That was so unjust! Zeus clenched his fists.

If he had to come face-to-face with King Cronus again to rescue his mother, then that's what he would do! As soon as he got the chance.

Around midnight the four Olympians neared the village where they'd last seen Hera and Demeter. They bedded down under some trees by the road near the village entrance.

At dawn they woke to the sound of familiar voices. *Hera and Demeter!* The two girls were walking toward them along the main road. Zeus and the others scrambled to their feet and went to meet them.

"Hestia!" Hera and Demeter squealed when they caught sight of her with the boys.

Hestia quickly handed off the lamp to Hades. Only Zeus seemed to notice that the flame instantly went dim again. The three girls jumped up and down and hugged one another.

"We were just coming to look for you," Hera told the boys after the girls had calmed down a little. "We didn't expect to find you so fast!"

"Look what we have," said Demeter. She reached into a bag she was carrying. She pulled out a long metal cone decorated with beautiful carvings. It's top was shaped like a shallow bowl.

"It's the torch!" Hera exclaimed.

Hades showed them the lamp. "And we've got the flame!"

Zeus's brow wrinkled. "But how do we know it's the right torch?"

"Of course it is," said Hera. "A priestess gave it to us."

"She said it came from a temple in Olympia," said Demeter. "One that Hyperion took over in King Cronus's name—"

"And guess what?" Hera broke in. "Before the Titans took over the temple, it was named the Temple of *Hera*." Her blue eyes gleamed. "Which must mean that the Olympic Torch is *my* magical object."

Demeter looked unsure. "Maybe." She glanced back at the others. "Anyway, Hyperion tried to force the priestess to hand over the Olympic Torch."

Hera picked up the story again. "But afraid of

what he'd do with it, the priestess tricked him. She separated the flame and torch, knowing that they only had true magical powers when united. She put the flame atop a regular torch and gave that to him instead."

"Then she fled the temple with this unlit magical torch we found," Demeter said. "When we told her about Pythia and our quest, she gave it to us. But she cautioned us that only the Protector of the Hearth can reunite the torch and flame again."

"What are we waiting for?" asked Hades. He held up the lamp. "Somebody try it and see what happens."

"I'll light it," Hera said eagerly. Reluctantly Demeter handed her the big, unlit torch. Taking great care, Hera held the torch over the lamp's flame.

Everyone leaned in, hardly daring to breathe.

Would the torch catch fire? Moments passed. The torch remained dark. The flame still burned dimly in the lamp.

Hera stared at the torch. Her shoulders slumped with disappointment. "What's wrong with this thing?"

"Let me try," Demeter said, reaching for the torch and lamp. But she had no more luck than Hera.

"Maybe the priestess made a mistake," said Hera. "Maybe this isn't the right torch after all."

"May I try?" asked Hestia. Her voice was gentle so as not to rub it in that her friends had failed. Yet there was a spark of excitement in it.

Demeter shrugged. "Sure. Go ahead." She passed the torch and lamp to Hestia.

The moment Hestia held the lamp close to the torch, the flame leaped to it. Everyone gasped as the torch immediately sparked high. Dazzling red, yellow, and blue lights wove together in a fiery dance. The six Olympians stared at the blazing torch in awe.

"Congratulations!" said an approving voice.

They'd all been so amazed by the torch that they hadn't noticed the vent that had opened in the ground behind them. In a glittering cloud of steam, the oracle Pythia's bespectacled face now rose before them.

CHAPTER TEN

Seeds of a New Quest

Hestia stared, wide-eyed, at the vision of Pythia. Clasping the torch to her chest, she took a step back.

"Oracle," Demeter whispered to her quickly.

"Oh," Hestia whispered back. "She's who you've all been talking about!"

"Well done, Olympians!" the oracle said. "You have united flame and torch and reclaimed the Olympic Torch at last. And now it is in

the hands of the Protector of the Hearth." She smiled at Hestia.

It was just as Zeus had suspected the moment he'd first handed the lamp to Hestia. That's why the torch had flamed higher and brighter for her than for anyone else. *She* was the Protector of the Hearth.

"The torch has great magic," Pythia told the Olympians. "And its flame can never die out. Already, in villages and towns across Earth, the torch's healing magic is causing people to return to their homes, their hearts filled with new hope for a better life."

She paused, peering out at them through her foggy spectacles. "Along with your other magical objects, this torch will serve you well and help you to help others in the difficult times to come. Especially as you continue to search for the remaining Olympians."

Zeus looked at her in surprise. "Remaining Olympians? But I thought there were only six of us. Me, Poseidon, Hades, Hera, Demeter, and Hestia. We're all here. Are you saying there are more?"

Pythia's eyes filled with a faraway look. Like she was remembering a truth that only she knew. "Yes. Cronus didn't swallow all of the Olympians," she replied mysteriously. "And so, you see, the quest must continue. For there are many more of you."

"How many?" asked Poseidon.

"But I was planning to search for—," Zeus started to say.

"Your mother is not in immediate danger," Pythia interrupted, answering Zeus. It wasn't the first time she'd seemed to read his mind. "You must gather the other Olympians before you seek her out."

She glanced at Poseidon. "As for their number, it is unclear to me at present."

Before Zeus could protest, or even ask his mother's name, Pythia threw her arms wide.

"Hyperion's actions have devastated the land," she said in a dramatic voice. "On your next quest you must repair it as best you can. You must find the Magic Seeds that will give this land new life."

"Where? How?" asked Hades.

"Use the magic you've already been given," she replied.

"Even if we repair the land, won't Hyperion just wreck it again with his fireballs?" asked Hera.

Pythia shook her head. "King Cronus wasn't happy to learn of your escape. Or that you'd reclaimed the flame. He blames Hyperion for losing the magic flame to you and has banished him." Her image in the steam wavered and began to fade.

"Wait! Don't go yet," Zeus called out. "Even if I must wait to see her, can you at least tell me my mother's name?"

"Mia," said Pythia, her image growing stronger again. "Or, hmm. Maybe it's Dia. Or Rhea. Or Leah. It's hazy. . . ." Then abruptly she disappeared.

"Hey, watch it, Hestia!" Poseidon complained suddenly.

"Oops. Sorry," she said. She'd put the bottom tip of her torch in the center of her palm and had set the torch spinning. While trying to balance it there, she'd accidentally bumped into him.

Zeus glimpsed Hera and Demeter watching her. Demeter's arms were crossed in front of her chest. And there was a pinched expression on Hera's face. Were they feeling jealous of Hestia? Like the boys, she had a magical object now. But the other two girls still hadn't earned theirs.

By now people who had long been away from home were gathering in the village center. "Something's changed," Zeus heard a woman say cheerfully. "I feel hopeful again. And glad to be home."

Another man nodded. "Me too. Though a great big thunderstorm would be nice. To make things grow again."

A *thunder*storm? thought Zeus. Pythia had said they should help repair the devastated land. *Use the magic you've already been given,* she'd said.

Zeus pulled Bolt from his belt. "Large!" he commanded. In an instant the thunderbolt expanded to its full length. Zeus drew back his arm. Then he sent Bolt flying toward the only cloud in the sky.

When the thunderbolt hit the cloud there was a loud crash. The sky darkened. Other clouds formed. Sparking and sizzling, Bolt zoomed from one cloud to another. Soon booms of thunder and flashes of lightning filled the entire sky.

All at once the heavy clouds dumped their precious load.

The Olympians and villagers dashed for cover as rain fell everywhere. It drummed the roofs of the houses. It fed the parched fields. And it collected in all the pots and urns around the well. And yet it didn't even dim the flaming torch that Hestia still held.

Having done its work, Bolt zoomed back to Zeus. The clouds stopped raining.

Awestruck and grateful, the villagers cheered

the Olympians. "Hooray! Thank you!" they cried out.

Would his mother have been proud of him if she could have seen what he had accomplished? Zeus wondered. He knew that more would be needed to heal the land. But this was a start. Next they needed to find those seeds Pythia had spoken of.

"Where to now, Thunderboy?" Hera asked. She was smiling at him for once, seeming pleased at what he'd done. They were all feeling pretty good now, having successfully completed their quest and having brought rain to the villagers.

"I'll check," said Zeus. But before he could fish his amulet from around his neck, a sound like the rumble of a hundred speeding chariots met the Olympians' ears.

They all turned toward the sound in surprise.

In the distance a great mound of earth had formed. Suddenly the mound exploded like a volcano.

The Olympians and villagers gasped. As they watched, a giant beanstalk pushed out of the crater where the mound had been. Quickly it sprouted up to the sky until it's tip-top disappeared into the clouds.

"Clamoring clams, that's one fast-growing plant!" Poseidon exclaimed.

Zeus grinned. "And you know what? I'm guessing it grew from a *Magic Seed*."

"Only one thing to do, right?" said Hades.

"Climb it!" they all cheered.

With their sights set on the distant beanstalk, the Olympians set off together on their next adventure.

THE OLYMPIANS CLIMB TO NEW HEIGHTS IN THE NEXT HEROES IN TRAINING ADVENTURE!

Join Zeus and his friends as they set off on the adventure of a lifetime.

EBOOK EDITIONS ALSO AVAILABLE
From Aladdin • KIDS.SimonandSchuster.com